The BACKYARDIGANS

Pirate Treasure

adapted by Justin Spelvin
based on the original teleplay by McPaul Smith
illustrated by Matthew Stoddart

SIMON AND SCHUSTER/NICKELODEON

Based on the TV series *Nick Jr. The Backyardigans*™ as seen on Nick Jr.

SIMON AND SCHUSTER
First published in Great Britain in 2007 by Simon & Schuster UK Ltd
Africa House, 64-78 Kingsway, London WC2B 6AH

Originally published in the USA in 2006 by Simon Spotlight,
an imprint of Simon & Schuster Children's Division, New York.

A CIP catalogue record for this book is available from the British Library

ISBN-10: 184738028X
ISBN-13: 9781847380289

Printed in China

10 9 8 7 6 5 4 3 2 1

Visit our websites: www.simonsays.co.uk
                          www.nickjr.co.uk

It was a perfect day for an adventure. Uniqua decided to be a pirate!

"Arrrr!" she said. "I'm Captain Uniqua."

She drew a big pirate flag in the sandbox.

"I'm Captain Austin with a hook for a hand!" Austin announced. He showed Uniqua his hook.

"Two pirates are better than one," said Uniqua. "Let's hunt for treasure together. I have half a treasure map, matey!"

"Arrrr!" Captain Austin answered. "Let's go!"

"Pirates!" Pablo said, pointing to the sand. "Pirates were here!"
"Can we be pirates too?" asked Tyrone. "I'll be Captain Tyrone with a wooden ear!"

"Arrrr!" said Pablo. "And I'm Captain Pablo with the peg leg!"
The two new pirates sailed their ship across the ocean.
"Arrrr! I see another ship," Tyrone called. "Let's raid it! That's what scurvy pirates do!"

Pablo and Tyrone climbed aboard the other ship and bumped right into Captain Uniqua and Captain Austin!

"Arrrr!" said Pablo. "Time to walk the plank."

"Hey, that sounds like fun!" said Uniqua. She and Austin jumped onto the plank with a laugh.

Uniqua and Austin walked off the plank . . . but they didn't splash into water. They landed in soft, soft sand!

"It's a desert island," said Uniqua. "Just like on our half of the treasure map!"

"We have half a treasure map too!" called Tyrone.
That gave Austin an idea.

"Maybe we should be one big band of pirates and put our halves of the map together," said Austin.

They put the two halves of the map together . . . and then they had a whole map!

"Look!" Uniqua said, pointing. "That *X* marks the spot where the treasure is buried."

The four pirates followed the map. They walked and walked.

Finally they came to a bubbling, stinky mud pit.

"It looks a little far to jump," said Austin.

"I think I see a way," said Uniqua. "We can walk across that tree."

"But I'm a peg-legged pirate," said Pablo. "Balancing is going to be tricky!"

Pablo took a small step. Then another. Then another. He was almost there!

But then he started to wobble. Pablo was going to fall!
"Arrrr!" cheered Tyrone. "You can do it!"

The three other pirates rushed over. They pulled Pablo to safety.
"Arrrr! Thanks, guys!" Pablo said.
"Arrrr! No problem," said the pirates.

The map said the *X* was nearby.
"I found a *V*," said Pablo.
"This one is a *W*," called Austin.
"Arrrr! Over here!" said Uniqua. "I found the *X*!"

They each took turns digging. Suddenly Uniqua hit something very hard.

"It's a treasure chest!" she called.
They pulled it out of the ground and opened the lid.

"It's the biggest diamond ever!" said Pablo.
"All in favour of sharing it, say 'Arrrr!'" said Uniqua.
"Arrrr!" cheered the pirates.
"But first let's bury it here," said Uniqua, "so that other pirates can't steal it."

"We can use the map to find it later," said Tyrone. "Let's mark the spot with a *Y*. No one will ever think of looking for a *Y*."

They quickly buried the treasure.

When the treasure was buried, the pirates stood and admired their work.

"All this pirating has made me hungry," said Uniqua. "All in favour of a snack, say 'Arrrr!'"

"Arrrr!" cheered Pablo, Austin, and Tyrone.

So the pirates headed home for a snack.